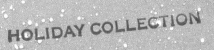

For Janice

Library of Congress Cataloging-in-Publication Data
Brown, Ken (Ken James).
Mucky Pup's Christmas/by Ken Brown.—1st American ed.
p. cm.
Summary: When Mucky Pup is banished from the farmhouse for
"spoiling" Christmas, he spends the night in the barn with the other
animals, thinking that Christmas does not seem like much fun.
ISBN 0-525-46141-8 (hc)
[1. Dogs—Fiction. 2. Christmas—Fiction.] I. Title.
PZ7.B8157Muf   1999   [E]—dc21   98-47019   CIP   AC

Published in the United States 1999 by Dutton Children's Books,
a division of Penguin Putnam Books for Young Readers
345 Hudson Street, New York, New York 10014
http://www.penguinputnam.com/yreaders/index.htm

Originally published in Great Britain 1998
by Andersen Press Ltd., London
Typography by Alan Carr • Printed in Italy
First American Edition
2   4   6   8   10   9   7   5   3   1

Mucky Pup's Christmas

by Ken Brown

Dutton Children's Books
NEW YORK

But no one appreciated his help.

"Bad, *bad* Mucky Pup! You've ruined the Christmas cards!" his family scolded.

"The Christmas cake is a mess, and look what you did to the beautiful tree. You've ruined everything, and Christmas is tomorrow. Out, Mucky Pup! Out of the house!"

Mucky Pup felt terrible.
He wandered out to the barn
to find his friend Pig.

"You sure look gloomy," said Pig. "What's up?"
"My family doesn't love me anymore," said Mucky
Pup miserably. "They say I've spoiled this Christmas
thing. Do you know what Christmas is, Pig?"

Pig didn't know. Neither did Horse, Hen, or Duck.
Cat *said* she knew but wasn't telling.

"It doesn't sound like much fun, whatever it is," said
Pig. "Cheer up, Mucky Pup. Stay here with us tonight."

So Mucky Pup settled down in the straw next to Pig. He missed his family and his warm bed by the fireplace. Once he thought he could hear someone calling his name, but perhaps it was just a dream.

The next morning, everything looked clean
and white and new.

"Do you think *this* is the Christmas thing, Pig?" asked Mucky Pup.

"Can't be," said Pig. "It looks like too much fun. Come on, Mucky
Pup. Let's play!"

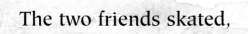

The two friends skated,

they snowballed,

and they sledded. Suddenly,
Mucky Pup lost his balance.

He tumbled down the hill toward the children and their snowman. He rolled faster and faster. **Wheeeeeeee!**

CRASH!

"Mucky Pup! You found us! We called and called, but you
never came home. Don't you know it's Christmas Day?"

The children put Mucky Pup on the sled and hurried home through the snow.

When he trotted into the warm farmhouse, his family patted his soft fur and scratched behind his ears. They fed him a delicious dinner and let him tumble and roll in the big pile of crumpled wrapping paper. There was even a present just for him.

So *this* is Christmas, and I didn't ruin it! thought Mucky Pup happily. He snuggled down in his own soft bed by the fire. He couldn't wait to tell Pig that Christmas turned out to be *lots* of fun after all.